This book belongs to:

_____

Biscuit's
CHRISTMAS STORYBOOK FAVORITES

by Alyssa Satin Capucilli   pictures by Pat Schories

HARPER
An Imprint of HarperCollinsPublishers

All rights reserved. Manufactured in China. For information address HarperCollins
Children's Books, a division of HarperCollins Publishers, 195 Broadway, New York,
NY 10007.
www.harpercollinschildrens.com
ISBN 978-0-06-304120-2
Book design by Brenda E. Angelilli
20 21 22 23 24 SCP 10 9 8 7 6 5 4 3 2 1
❖
Revised edition, 2020

Biscuit's
CHRISTMAS STORYBOOK FAVORITES

Table of Contents

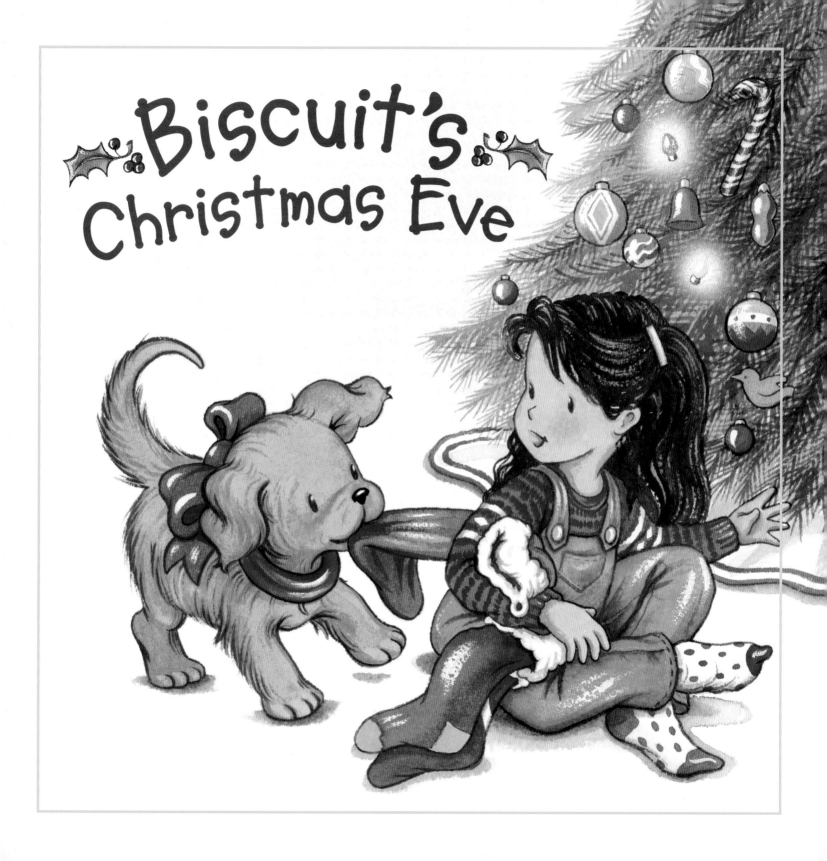

Biscuit's
Christmas Eve

"It's Christmas Eve, Biscuit."

Woof, woof!

"It's the night before Christmas, and we have lots to do."

Woof!

"Our Christmas tree is trimmed
with beautiful decorations.

Which one is your favorite, Biscuit?"

Woof, woof!

"Funny puppy!
That decoration looks just
like your ball!"

Woof!

"It's time to hang the Christmas stockings, Biscuit.

Soon Santa Claus will fill them with wonderful treats!"

"This one says, Biscuit!"

Woof, woof!

"Silly puppy!

Come back with that stocking!"

Woof!

"It's fun to make a Christmas gift for friends and family, Biscuit.

Mom and Dad will love this painting of us!

Now, where can the wrapping paper be?"

Woof, woof!

"Oh, Biscuit.

You found the

wrapping paper . . .

. . . and the ribbon!"

Woof!

"Listen, Biscuit!
Do you hear
what I hear?"

Woof, woof!
Woof, woof!

"It's the
Christmas carolers!
Let's sing along!
Fa la la la la!"
Woof!

"It just wouldn't be Christmas without cookies
and milk for Santa Claus and his reindeer, Biscuit."
Woof, woof!

"*M-m-m.*

They smell delicious!"

Woof!

"Don't worry, Biscuit!

There's a treat for you, too!"

Woof!

21

"We're all ready, Biscuit.
I can hardly wait
for Christmas!"
Woof, woof!

"Curl up, Biscuit.
Let's share a Christmas
story while we wait
for Santa Claus!"
Woof!

Z-z-z-z-z!
Z-z-z-z-z!

23

"Hooray! Wake up, sleepy puppy!

Christmas is here at last!"

Woof, woof! Woof, woof!

"Oh, Biscuit. The very best part of Christmas is sharing it with a sweet puppy like you!"
Woof, woof!

"Merry Christmas, Biscuit!"

"Biscuit, where are you?"

Woof, woof!

"Come along, sweet puppy!

Today is a very special day.

We're going on a trip.

We're going to visit with our family."

Woof, woof!

"Let's get ready, Biscuit.

First we must pack our bags. I'll take my favorite doll."

Woof, woof!

"And you have your blanket and your bone."

Woof!

"It's fun to take a trip, Biscuit.

The car ride may be long, but we can share stories and sing songs."

Woof, woof!

"Even the baby can sing along!"

"This map shows us just where we are going, Biscuit.

There's so much to see along the way."

Woof, woof!

"Funny puppy!

You found some horses and cows already!"

Woof!

"Look, Biscuit.

There are tall mountains, rolling hills, and lots of trees."

Woof, woof!

"This is a perfect spot to stretch our legs."

Woof, woof!

"What have you found now, Biscuit?"

"Hooray! We're here at last.

There's Grandma and Grandpa."

Woof, woof!

"Aunt Clara, Uncle Henry, and our cousins are here, too.

We're going to have lots of fun on this trip!"

Woof, woof!

"Come along, everybody.

It's time to go sledding!"

Woof, woof!

"Hold on, Biscuit.

Off we go!"

Woof, woof!

"We can go ice skating on the pond, too."

Woof, woof!

"Oh, no!

Silly puppy. Be careful!

The ice is too slippery for you."

Woof!

"This way, Biscuit.

We'll take a long walk through the woods.

I have my binoculars."

Woof, woof!

"And you have a pinecone!"

Woof!

"Let's warm up by the fire, Biscuit.

There's hot apple cider, doughnuts . . ."

Woof, woof!

". . . and a bone just for you!"

Woof, woof!

"Now it's time for a special family treat!

We're going on a sleigh ride.

Cuddle up, sweet puppy.

It's beginning to snow!"

Woof, woof!

"There's nothing quite like spending time with our family, is there, Biscuit?"

Woof, woof!

"Smile everyone. This is one trip we'll always want to remember!"

Woof, woof!

Biscuit's Christmas

"Come along, Biscuit," called the little girl.

"Christmas is almost here.

It's time to choose our tree."

Woof, woof!

"This tree is just the right size, Biscuit."

Woof, woof!

"Oh, Biscuit! You found a pinecone!"

"Mmm-mm! I smell hot chocolate!"

Woof, woof!

"Silly puppy!

How did you get those marshmallows?"

"We have everything we need
to trim the tree, Biscuit.
We have our friends, our family,
and lots of decorations."

Woof, woof!

"No, no, Biscuit!"

Bow wow!

"No tugging, Puddles!

The popcorn is for the tree!"

"It's time to put the star at the very top!"

Woof, woof!

"Wait, Biscuit!

Come back with that candy cane!"

"The stockings are hung.

Let's have some apple cider

and sing Christmas carols!"

Woof, woof!

"Biscuit, what are you doing?"

Woof, woof!

"Funny puppy, you are right!

I almost forgot to leave gingerbread and milk

for Santa Claus!"

"Oh, Biscuit, don't you just love the sweet smell of Christmas?"

Biscuit Finds a Friend

Woof! Woof!

What has Biscuit found?

Is it a ball?

Woof!

Is it a bone?

Woof!

Quack!

It is a little duck.

The little duck is lost.

Woof! Woof!

We will bring the little duck
back to the pond.

Woof! Woof!

Here, little duck.

Here is the pond.

Here are your mother
and your father.

Quack!

Here are your brothers
and your sisters.
Quack! Quack!

The ducks say thank you.

Thank you for finding

the little duck.

Quack!

The little duck

wants to play.

Quack!

Woof!

Quack!

Woof!

Splash!

Biscuit fell into the pond!

Silly Biscuit.

You are all wet!

Woof!

Oh no, Biscuit.

Not a big shake!

Woof!

Time to go home, Biscuit.

Quack! Quack!

Say good-bye, Biscuit.

Woof! Woof!

Good-bye, little duck.

Biscuit has found

a new friend.

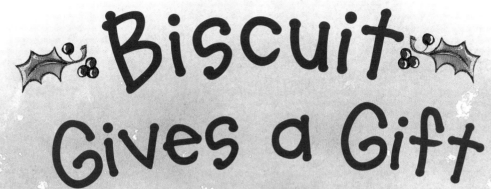

Biscuit Gives a Gift

"Wake up, sleepy puppy!
It's Christmas, and we
have lots to do."
Woof, woof!

"We're going to give some special gifts

to our neighbors, friends, and family, Biscuit."

Woof, woof!

"Oh, Biscuit! Wait for me."

Woof!

"These mittens are so warm and cozy.

We can hang them on the mitten tree."

Woof, woof!

"Silly puppy!

No tugging, Biscuit."

"This way, Biscuit.

Grandma and Grandpa will love

the gingerbread we baked."

Woof, woof!

"Funny puppy!

No cookies for you!"

Woof!

"Sharing a story is one of the best gifts of all."

Woof, woof!

"Curl up, Biscuit. You
can hear the story, too."
Woof!

"Gifts come in all shapes
and sizes, Biscuit.
We can give birdseed to the birds."

"And big crunchy biscuits to friends like Puddles and Sam."

Woof, woof!

"Sweet puppy!
A kiss from you is the best
Christmas gift ever!"
Woof!

Biscuit's Day at the Farm

Come along, Biscuit.
We are going to help
on the farm today.

Woof! Woof!

We can feed the hens, Biscuit.

Woof, woof!

We can feed the pigs, too.

The pigpen

is empty, Biscuit.

Where can the pigs be?

Woof, woof!

Funny puppy.

You found the pig
and the piglets, too.
Woof!

Let's feed the goats,

Biscuit.

Woof, woof!

Oink!

Oh, Biscuit.

The piglet is out of the pen.

We must put the piglet back.

Woof, woof!

Let's feed the sheep, Biscuit.

Woof, woof!

Oink!

Oh no, Biscuit.

It's the piglet!

We must put the piglet back
one more time.
Woof, woof!

Here are the geese,
Biscuit.

Woof, woof!

Oink!

Here is the piglet again.

Woof, woof!

Oink, oink!

Honk!

Wait, Biscuit!
The geese are just
saying hello.

Woof!

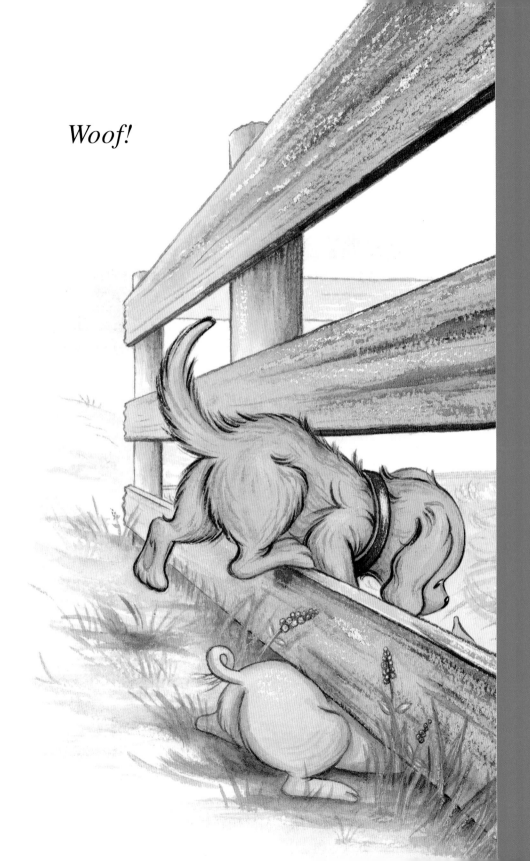

Silly puppy!
The piglet is back
in the pen.

And so are you, Biscuit!

Oink!

Woof, woof!

Biscuit's Snowy Day

"Come along, Biscuit. It's snowing!

We're going to have a great snowy day!"

Woof, woof!

"I'll put on my mittens and boots."

Woof, woof!

"And here's a cozy sweater for you.

Let's go, sweet puppy!"

Woof!

"We're all going to build a snowman, Biscuit.

Everyone can help roll a big, big snowball!"

Woof, woof!

"Funny puppy!

That's the way!"

Woof!

"Oh, Biscuit!

You found the snowman's scarf and hat!"

Woof, woof!

"You found his carrot nose, too!

What do you think, Biscuit?"

Woof!

"The snow is so soft and powdery.

It's perfect for making snow angels."

"And snow puppies, too."

Woof, woof!

Bow, wow!

141

"Look, Biscuit. It's time to go sledding!

Hold on tight, sweet puppy."

Woof, woof!

"Here we go!"

Woof!

"There's nothing like a great snowy day, Biscuit.

There's hot cocoa and treats."

Woof, woof!

"And lots of fun for all!"

Biscuit and the Lost Teddy Bear

Woof, woof!

What do you see, Biscuit?

Is it a bird?

Woof, woof!

Is it a butterfly?

Woof, woof!

Oh, Biscuit.

It is a teddy bear!

Woof, woof!

Somebody lost a teddy bear.

Who can it be?

Woof, woof!

Woof, woof!

Is this your teddy bear, Sam?

Ruff!

No. It is not Sam's bear.

Woof, woof!

Is this your teddy bear, Puddles?

Bow wow!

No. It is not Puddles's bear.

Woof, woof!

Someone lost a teddy bear.

But who can it be?

Woof, woof!

Wait, Biscuit.

What do you see now?

Woof!

Biscuit sees a big truck.

Woof!

Biscuit sees a lot of boxes.

Woof, woof!

Biscuit sees a little boy, too.

Woof, woof! Woof, woof!

Is this your teddy bear,

little boy?

Yes. It is!

Woof!

The little boy

lost his teddy bear, Biscuit,

but you found it!

Woof, woof!

The teddy bear gets a big hug.

Woof, woof!

And Biscuit gets a big hug, too!

Woof!

"Guess what time it is, Biscuit!" said the little girl.

Woof, woof!

"It's time to celebrate Christmas once again!"

Woof!

"Come along, Biscuit. We need to finish our present for Grandma and Grandpa."

Woof, woof!

"I hope they like this Christmas album we're making for them."

Woof!

"Hold still, Biscuit!
A picture of you in front
of the Christmas tree is
just what we need."
Woof, woof!

"Silly puppy! That candy cane

belongs on the tree!" *Woof!*

"Tonight, we'll sing Christmas carols."

Woof, woof!

"Let's take a picture by the piano."

Woof!

"Oh, Biscuit! I can hardly wait to sing carols, too."

Woof!

"Here are the stockings, hung by the chimney with care."

Woof, woof!

"Oh, no! How did you get
that stocking?" *Woof!*

"We need to leave gingerbread and milk for Santa Claus."

Woof, woof!

"Funny puppy! That gingerbread is for Santa!" *Woof!*

Ding dong!

"There's the door, Biscuit!

Let's go!"

Woof, woof!

"Merry Christmas, Grandma and Grandpa!"

Woof!

"From both of us!"

"There's nothing better than celebrating Christmas with our family, our friends, and a silly little puppy like you, Biscuit!"

Woof, woof!

"Smile, Biscuit! Merry Christmas!"

Woof!

Merry Christmas! *Woof!*

The End

HARPER
An Imprint of HarperCollins Publishers

www.harpercollinschildrens.com   Illustrations © Pat Schories